Exploring
Beedle the Bard

I0614933

Unauthorized, pithy, tale-by-tale perspectives

By Dr Graeme Davis

NIMBLE BOOKS LLC

NIMBLE BOOKS LLC

ISBN-13: 978-1-934840-79-5

ISBN-10: 1-934840-79-3

Copyright 2009 Graeme Davis

Last saved 12/12/2008 3:51 PM

Nimble Books LLC

1521 Martha Avenue

Ann Arbor, MI 48103-5333

http://www.nimblebooks.com

The cover font, heading fonts and the body text inside the book are in Constantia, designed by John Hudson for Microsoft.

Contents

NIMBLE BOOKS LLC

THE TALES OF BEEDLE THE BARD—A BOOK WORTH EXPLORING

The Tales of Beedle the Bard is something rather more than just an ordinary book. One writer has hit the nail on the head by calling it an artifact. This book started life as a fictitious plot element in J. K. Rowling's *Harry Potter and the Deathly Hallows*, but it is now an actual, real-world book. Something which existed only in the imaginary world of Harry Potter has been made real.

What we have been given is a very special book at two levels. First it will make a tangible difference in our world through the profits that will go to a children's charity, offering the hope of a better future to many thousands of children. The financial support that will be made available to vulnerable children through the publication of *The Tales of Beedle the Bard* is substantial, with the prospect of transformed lives and a better world. Second is the value of these moral fables in giving all readers a framework for developing understanding of the great questions of human existence. Through the ages, myths and fables have done just this, and the triumph of J. K. Rowling is to produce a set of five moral fables for our age that are not in an old and unread book sitting on a dusty shelf in a library but actually read and talked about by millions of children and adults. Very few books have the potential for good of *The Tales of Beedle the Bard*.

It is in *Harry Potter and the Deathly Hallows* that we first hear of the book. By his will Albus Dumbledore bequeaths a copy of the first edition to Hermione Granger, knowing that they will help them understand what the Deathly Hallows are, and ultimately help in the defeat of Voldemort. One of the stories—*The Tale of the Three Brothers*—is told in full within the novel, and there is extensive discussion of it. Three of the other four tales are named.

The Children's High Level Group

Profits from sales of J. K. Rowling's book *The Tales of Beedle the Bard* will be donated to the charity The Children's High Level Group (CHLG), which "campaigns to protect and promote children's rights and make life better for vulnerable young people." The charity was set up in 2005 by J. K. Rowling and Baroness Nicholson of Winterbourne MEP. There is information about CHLG in a letter from Baroness Nicholson published at the back of *The Tales of Beedle the Bard*, and this letter is well worth reading. More information about CHLG is available at their website www.chlg.org including information about getting involved in their work.

Publication History

The Tales of Beedle the Bard has now been published in two editions, with the second edition in a collector's and a standard format.

The first edition (2007) was limited to just seven copies, each one hand-written by J. K. Rowling with her hand-drawn illustrations. Now writing that lot out seven times must have been worse than writing lines for Severus Snape! Each one was bound in brown, morocco leather, and each one decorated by silversmiths Hamilton & Inches of Edinburgh with five silver pieces representing the five tales, and each has its own, unique semi-precious stone. These are very special books, more like mediaeval manuscripts of the pre-print age than the mass produced editions usual today.

J. K. Rowling has explained the concept behind the seven books in these terms:

> *The idea came really because I wanted to thank six key people who have been very closely connected to the "Harry Potter" series, and these were people for whom a piece of*

jewelry wasn't going to cut it. So I had the idea of writing them a book, a handwritten and illustrated book, just for these six people. And well, if I'm doing six I really have to do seven, and the seventh book will be for this cause, which is so close to my heart.

Of the six books written to thank key people, the identities of the owners of two have been revealed. These are Barry Cunningham, J. K. Rowling's first editor, and Arthur A Levine, the editor of the American Harry Potter publisher Scholastic. The other four copies are out there, somewhere!

The seventh copy, the magical number seven auctioned for charity, is decorated with a moonstone and is therefore known as *The Moonstone Edition*. This book—perhaps a better word is indeed artifact as used in the auction catalogue—was auctioned by the London auction house Sothebys on 13th December 2007. It had a reserve price of £30,000 ($45,000). There were high hopes that it might reach £50,000 ($75,000).

No-one, just no-one, guessed the price it ultimately went for. The price was £1,950,000—that's $3,000,000 or more. This is the highest price ever for a modern, literary manuscript, and a truly incredible price for what is in the end a short manuscript in a nice binding. The Moonstone Edition was bought by Amazon.com. Access to this remarkable book is inevitably limited, but there are occasions when Amazon.com has made access available. There are some lucky fans who have seen and touched this remarkable manuscript.

There it might have ended. However, that leaves out of consideration the clamor of J. K. Rowling's fans, and it is the fans who prompted J. K. Rowling to publish a popular edition. Fans wanted to read these tales, yet it seemed that this was only possible by gaining access to one of the seven copies, which for most fans meant simply meant it wasn't going to happen. While a few notes appeared on web sites setting out in a paragraph or two the plot of the tales this really wasn't adequate, and J. K. Rowling conceded that her fans had a point. A conventional, mass publication did seem in order. Now for those without a couple of million of pounds in their piggy bank we have a second edition (2008) in the form of two more modestly priced versions. There is a limited edition Collectors' Edition—limited to 100,000 copies, which is in fact a very big limited edition—and the standard edition, which is a modest and very affordable hardback.

The illustrations reproduced in the book are drawn by J. K. Rowling herself, and they add a personal touch. They are not great works of art, but they are products of the author and give us some hints as to how she visualizes the stories. In the Harry Potter books we have illustrations by a professional artist, but whether they truly represent J. K. Rowling's vision we can never know. For example Severus Snape is pictured with a beard, yet there is no reference in the text of the books to him having a beard. By contrast the illustrations in *The Tales of Beedle the Bard* are part of the J. K. Rowling cannon. If J. K. Rowling draws something, that must be how she sees it. Her artwork is on the cover also—and curiously the UK and US versions have different cover pictures.

So today we have *The Tales of Beedle the Bard*, an artifact ripped from the pages of *Harry Potter and the Deathly Hallows*, made famous through its seven handwritten books, and now at a bookshop near you.

WHY BEEDLE THE BARD?

The Tales of Beedle the Bard are presented as if they are a collection of tales handled by the "real" characters of Albus Dumbledore and Hermione Granger. But of course Albus Dumbledore and Hermione Granger are themselves fictitious characters. What we have is something like a television programme as a plot device within a television programme, here a book within a book. Through this double layer of fiction we approach the character that is Beedle the Bard, and we are asked to believe in him, to consider that he really did exist, living in Yorkshire in the fifteenth century.

Beedle is not an established first name in English. Quite why J. K. Rowling used this name is not clear. It may perhaps echo the name Bede, the great Northumbria writer and historian who preserved many stories relating to the earliest history of the English people. Or she may be seeing it as the surname Beedle, which is indeed an old Yorkshire family name—a name therefore from the very county where J. K. Rowling tells us Beedle lived.

Within the English literary tradition "the Bard" is simply William Shakespeare and absolutely no-one else, yet a comparison of Beedle with William Shakespeare does not seem either intended or helpful. Rather the idea behind the name "bard" seems to be simply someone whose profession is storyteller, though the word "bard" in this meaning is scarcely used in English today. A thousand years ago or thereabouts England was full of bards, and it may be that we should see Beedle as part of this tradition. There are closer parallels to Beedle within the Welsh custom of appointing national bards, something which continues today. We should remember that J. K. Rowling grew up on the borders of Wales, and may well be familiar with the concept. Wales places enormous cultural importance on its long tradition of stories and songs often remembered through an oral tradition, and Wales is a milieu in which the Beedle we are shown would fit comfortably.

The Tales of Beedle the Bard is (or so we are asked to believe) part of a European tradition of collections of fairy tales. For J. K. Rowling as a scholar of French literature at the University of Exeter this must mean that she sees Beedle as a part of the tradition which includes Jean de la Fontaine (1621-1695), whose *Fables* and *Contes* (Stories) have been enduringly popular. No-one in Britain studies French literature even at secondary school level without being exposed to la Fontaine, and his short stories have become a standard school-room exercise in translation. Despite this rough treatment he rarely fails to impress. Through la Fontaine's work we can glimpse a plethora of earlier tellers of fairy tales within the European tradition: Aesop and Horace from the Classical world, Boccacio, Ariosto and Tasso from Italy. All these may be seen as influences either directly or at the one remove of la Fontaine on J. K. Rowling in her writing of these five tales. Yet there are more recent influences also.

The best known collection of such traditional tales is that made in Germany by the Brothers Grimm—Jacob and Wilhelm—and published by them in the early nineteenth century. Stories they recorded and that without their work may otherwise have been lost include *Rumpelstiltskin*, *Snow White*, *Sleeping Beauty*, *Cinderella* and *Hansel and Gretel*. These stories were once the staple of European bards, stories that had evolved over the centuries through an oral tradition, and were collected from traditional story-tellers and transferred to paper by the Brothers Grimm. Countless re-workings and retellings since their publication mean that these stories are today a part of the cultural heritage of Europe and North America. Hans Christian Andersen made a similarly large contribution to the stock of traditional tales. His *Fairy Tales* (published in installments 1835–1837) gave the world *The Little Mermaid*, *The Ugly Duckling*, *The Emperor's New Clothes* and *The*

Princess and the Pea. While he was subject to many folk influences in his native Denmark and more widely in Scandinavia, these stories were essentially composed by him—in contrast with the Brothers Grimm who were collecting stories. It is not made clear whether we should regard Beedle the Bard as like the Brothers Grimm as a collector of tales, or like Hans Christian Andersen as a writer of tales. Of course J. K. Rowling herself is acting as Andersen did.

Tales of Hoffmann (1881)—a title which may have influenced *The Tales of Beedle the Bard*—is an opera by Jacques Offenbach based on stories by E. T. A. Hoffmann. Hoffmann gave us tales including *The Nutcracker and the Mouse King*, *The Golden Pot* and *The Sandman*.

English is rich in traditional stories, though there is no single collection comparable to that made by the Brothers Grimm. Some are ancient, for example those around King Arthur (the once and future King) and King Alfred (who burnt the cakes). Others are around historic figures who may even have done something not wholly unlike the activities attributed to them—*Hereward the Wake*, *Old King Cole*, *Robin Hood*. Some are more obviously fairy tales—*Robin Goodfellow* (the troublesome elf) and the *Lambton Worm* come to mind. *Gog and Magog*, *Lady Godiva*, *Jack and the Beanstalk* and many, many more all have a long tradition in the English speaking world. Some traditional stories have been transformed into great works in English literature. Thus for example Edmund Spenser's *Faerie Queen* and Thomas Malory's *Le Morte d'Arthur* both develop the King Arthur tales and demonstrating that fairy stories can be transformed into world class literature.

Fairy tales can be a slippery concept to define, though usually the give-away is that magic is used. There is a particular problem in the case of *The Tales of Beedle the Bard* where they are set within a world—that of Harry Potter—where magic is held to exist, so it is not clear how the magic world could regard them as fairy stories. A partial answer is that four of the five tales flout the laws of magic as set out in the Harry Potter world, so that even within the concept of a magic world these tales are still magic. By contrast *Babbity Rabbitty and her Cackling Stump* keeps to the rules (with one possible exception—we seem to have an animagus speaking while transformed) and might appear as a story which makes no leap of belief and is not therefore a fairy story. Perhaps a better feel for what a fairy story is comes from J. R. R. Tolkien, who believes that these are stories which have a "certain mood and power" of Faerie. The mood and power of *The Tales of Beedle the Bard* does indeed seem to be that of fairy stories.

In our world the magic in fairy stories can be used to create mischief, but also to solve problems, and the resolutions of our fairy stories are usually magical. At the end there is a magic intervention and a solution appears. In *The Tales of Beedle the Bard* something rather different is happening. Magic may does not necessarily solve the problems—indeed the moral seems to be that we should look within ourselves for solutions.

WHO IS BEEDLE THE BARD?

We are told that Beedle the Bard is an historic figure living in England's Yorkshire in the fifteenth century. Two remarkable qualities about Beedle the Bard are presented—that he was a Muggle-lover, and that he was a feminist.

We are told that Beedle's age is one in which Muggles were persecuting witches and wizards, so the concept of a Muggle-loving wizard is particularly striking. It truly is a case of a man loving his enemy. Beedle therefore stands against the spirit of racism and hatred of his age, and can be an example for our age.

Beedle the feminist is a tougher idea. Feminism is a surprisingly modern concept, and carries with it a lot of baggage related to our society and our age. As an enormously powerful concept it is hard to summarize in a few words, yet, if pushed to try, it must surely be on the lines of a modern movement advocating equality between the sexes. A staple of high school literature essays is to look at the character of The Wife of Bath as presented by Geoffrey Chaucer in his *Canterbury Tales* and ask "was the Wife of Bath the first feminist?" Now Chaucer was a fourteenth century writer, and the effort to apply the modern concept of feminism to the fourteenth century quickly become problematic. Weaker students tend to say that the Wife of Bath is a strong female who stood up for herself against her husbands and who says that women want to be the masters, and because of this she must be a feminist. Stronger students point out that she should be judged by concepts of her own time, but in any case she is a violent husband-beater, and that this isn't feminism. Just as I'm not happy about arguing that Chaucer's Wife of Bath is a feminist, I am not happy about trying to argue that Beedle the Bard is a feminist. Certainly he has strong female roles in his stories, and many of his male characters do not behave well, but this is not feminism. In the stories possibly we might feel that aggressive women do well, and that meek women (as the Maiden in *The Warlock's Hairy Heart*) suffer, but again this is not feminism. Rather it seems to me that Beedle the Bard (and therefore J. K. Rowling) is simply an observer of life, and an observer of the roles of women and men.

WHAT DOES THIS BOOK OFFER?

The Tales of Beedle the Bard stand on their own, just as do any fairy tales or fables you might know. What *this* book offers is an assessment of the literary merits (and demerits) of each tale, along with some discussion of language and textual issues. For the fan of J. K. Rowling and *The Tales of Beedle the Bard* this book presents something which is thought-provoking. You might agree with my assessments (that would be nice!) but in a way I hope you don't! What I hope is that you will react to my views. Which tales do you think are strongest? What lesson for life do you take from the tales?

As well as commentary and assessment I've presented some background information which might help. Most of this is in the form of special sections at the end of each chapter. Sometimes I've suggested sources, or even criticized J. K. Rowlings (something sure to shock the fans, I know!) For example we are told the whole of the original tales was written in runes and that these have been translated by Hermione Granger, so I thought you might be interested in more information about runes, and why they cannot be translated.

We are told that the original of *The Tales of Beedle the Bard* was written in RUNES. Runes are the individual letters of the RUNIC ALPHABET used in the Middle Ages by people living in the north of Europe, particularly the Scandinavian peoples (including the Vikings) and the English. Runes and runic are *not* a language—for example it is perfectly possible to write English in the runic alphabet (as Beedle the Bard is supposed to have done) and it is still the English language. Hermione Granger studied runes and would know that runic is an alphabet not a language. She would therefore be horrified at the howler of a mistake printed on the title page of *The Tales of Beedle the Bard*: "Translated from the original runes by Hermione Granger." You can never translate from one alphabet to another, rather you transliterate one alphabet into another.

There are three main versions of the runic alphabet. The Elder Futhork—named for its first six letters F-U-TH-O-R-K (with the sound TH seen as one letter)—had twenty-four letters and was used in Scandinavia. The Old English runic alphabet was called the Futhark—with an A instead of an O—and had twenty-nine letters.

The last form of runic, mainly used in Scandinavia, was the Younger Futhork with just sixteen letters. All the alphabets could be supplemented by special characters with special meanings, so runes could get very complicated.

In England the runic alphabet went out of fashion around the seventh century AD, though runic was at least occasionally used until the sixteenth century in parts of Scandinavia, and even today many Scandinavians (especially Swedes) do know the names of the letters of the runic alphabet. The idea of Beedle the Bard in fifteenth century Yorkshire (England) using runes is a nice J. K. Rowling touch. Perhaps we are to imagine that he used the runic alphabet that really existed in the time when he is imagined as writing, the Younger Futhork.

In popular culture there are links between runes and fortune telling. The very word "rune" means "secret" or "hidden" in Old Norse (the old language of Scandinavia), though the idea seems to be that the runes hide within them words—or simply that it is possible to read them. The link of runes with magic and mystery seems to be a modern invention of a superstitious age. There is none of this nonsense in *The Tales of Beedle the Bard*, or indeed in the Harry Potter books.

FIFTEENTH CENTURY YORKSHIRE is an unlikely home for Beedle the Bard. Its associations are religious, military and dynastic, and magical connotations do not readily spring to mind. The county town of York is one of the two English archbishoprics (the other is Canterbury), a feature which encouraged a spirit of independence for the area. At the supposed time of Beedle the Bard England certainly ruled Yorkshire in name, but in lots of ways Yorkshire and the other northern English counties simply did what they wanted. This is a county from which massive armies were raised for the War of the Roses. In the fifteenth century the Dukes of York (the white rose) defeated their bitter enemies from the county next door the Dukes of Lancaster (the red rose) and seized the throne of England—only to lose it on the battlefield to a Lancastrian scion, King Henry VII. There are few specific magical associations for the county in the fifteenth century. For that matter Yorkshire does not feature in the Harry Potter novels, though the Hogwarts Express must pass through it two or three hours out from London Kings Cross. There doesn't seem to be a J. K. Rowlings association either.

The pretence that *The Tales of Beedle the Bard* existed before J. K. Rowling wrote them is a traditional literary device—indeed it is the cliché which starts most Gothic novels, and is of a type with the opening lines of novelist Horace Walpole's work of fiction *The Castle of Otranto*, which begins in the following terms:

The following work was found in the library of an ancient Catholic family in the north of England. It was printed at Naples, in the black letter, in the year 1529. How much sooner it was written does not appear. The principal incidents are such as were believed in the darkest ages of Christianity; but the language and conduct have nothing that savours of barbarism. The style is the purest Italian.

If the story was written near the time when it is supposed to have happened, it must have been between 1095, the era of the first Crusade, and 1243, the date of the last, or not long afterwards. There is no other circumstance in the work that can lead us to guess at the period in which the scene is laid: the names of the actors are evidently fictitious, and probably disguised on purpose: yet the Spanish names of the domestics seem to indicate that this work was not composed until the establishment of the Arragonian Kings in Naples had made Spanish appellations familiar in that country. The beauty of the diction, and the zeal of the author (moderated, however, by singular judgment) concur to make me think that the date of the composition was little antecedent to that of the impression. Letters were then in their most flourishing state in Italy, and contributed to dispel the empire of superstition, at that time so forcibly attacked by the reformers. It is not unlikely that an artful priest might endeavour to turn their own arms on the innovators, and might avail himself of his abilities as an author to confirm the populace in their ancient errors and superstitions. If this was his view, he has certainly acted with signal address. Such a work as the following would enslave a hundred vulgar minds beyond half the books of controversy that have been written from the days of Luther to the present hour.

This device of suggesting an origin for a work of fiction is rarely used today. A past age needed to feel they were reading something that was true; we are happy simply to read something that is entertaining. J. K. Rowling has given us a usage of this traditional device which is unusual for our age—and that she has made it work suggests her strength as a writer.

1. EXPLORING *THE WIZARD AND THE HOPPING POT*

STARS ★★★★★ (5/7)

The image of the Hopping Pot in this tale is great—but the moral of the story is very weak, for the young wizard does not seem to exhibit any inner learning. This tale is entertaining on first reading, but ultimately not satisfying.

PLOT

This story is about the legacy of a generous old wizard who had been in the habit of helping his Muggle neighbors, saying that the cures came from his magic cooking pot. On his death, he left all his belongings to his only son. Among the possessions bequeathed to him the son finds the cooking pot and a single slipper inside it, together with a note from his father that reads, "In the fond hope, my son, that you will never need this."

The son is without the generosity of his father, and he closes the door on every person who asks for his help. The first one seeking his aid is an old woman whose granddaughter is plagued with warts. Closing the door on the old woman, the son hears a clanking in the kitchen and sees his pot has grown a single foot and developed a bad case of warts. With its single foot it is indeed a hopping pot. The next one to look for his aid is an old man, whose donkey is lost or stolen, so that he cannot get to the market to fetch food for his starving family. The son closes the door on him too, and the pot starts making sounds like a donkey. A few more similar incidents take place, until the son finally gives up and calls all the neighbors to offer them help. As the people's troubles fade away, the pot empties, until at last out pops the mysterious slipper—one that perfectly fits the foot of the now-quiet pot, and together the two walk off, effectively into the sunset.

CHARACTERS

The good, old wizard.

His son the bad, young wizard.

Several villagers.

The Hopping Pot.

ILLUSTRATIONS

We see the Hopping Pot complete with warts and slugs and chasing after the young wizard—though only the wizard's feet and legs are seen. He is wearing shoes with the toes curling upwards, suggesting that J. K. Rowling envisages the action taking place in a time long ago. The conclusion of the story—the wizard and the hopping pot walking home—is also pictured. While there isn't a sunset the feel is very much that of "and they all lived happily ever after."

ASSESSMENT

This is on the surface a tidy and satisfying story. The young wizard is punished for his misdeeds until he decides to mend his ways. The woes of the villagers are all cured, and we last see the young wizard and the silenced hopping pot walking home together. We are told that for fear the hopping pot should one day cast off its slipper the son continues to help the villagers. In good, fairy-story fashion there is a happy ending for everyone.

Though in its framework it is tidy and satisfying, this tale is ultimately very weak. There is no sense of the young wizard seeing the error of his ways, and acting out of true generosity or compassion. Rather he is motivated by self interest to prevent the torments of the pot. Presumably the pot remains with him, ready to cast its slipper and start banging (and worse) at a moment's notice.

The old wizard has indeed found a clever way to make his son do the right thing, and there is no doubt that the villagers benefit from this. Yet the young wizard has not made the step of seeing his previous activities as wrong, and in this respect the moral is not adequately presented. A good tale should show us the value of doing the right thing because it is the right thing. This story shows us only the value of doing right to avoid punishment.

LESSONS FOR LIFE

Do good to others—or something nasty might happen to you. The lesson should be on the lines of, do good to others because that is the right thing to do, and Dumbledore's notes on the tale indeed point in this direction. Yet this is not the meaning of the tale as it is written. Indeed we seem to have some sort of invocation of *karma*, the Buddhist idea that if you do nasty things then nasty things will happen to you, while if you do good things then good things will happen to you.

At the start of the story the son considers the non-magic villagers to be worthless. He is making prejudiced judgments about his neighbors through what is a form of racism. The message of the story is that racism is wrong.

LANGUAGE

Hopping Pot is a well-established term in the English of South-East England. In origin a *hopping pot* is a large cooking pot used by families of Londoners during the six weeks or so they spent picking the hop harvest (hopping, or 'opping). In England hops are used to flavor beer, and are grown mainly in the South-Eastern counties of Kent, Surrey and Sussex (counties close to London). For poor Londoners picking them was a form of paid holiday, and 'opping *down Kent way* (hopping in Kent) was once a familiar part of London life. Families were accommodated either in tents or in huts, and cooking was done in a large, communal pot over an open fire— the hopping pot. The tradition of hop-picking is centuries old and continued at least until the 1970s (the process is now mechanized) and the idea of a hopping pot as a large cooking pot is well understood by London families.

Hopping Pot has undergone a special extension of meaning in London. London has produced a remarkable urban slang in Cockney Rhyming Slang, where familiar phrases are found which rhyme with a noun. So *Gypsy Rosie Lee* (a lady very famous in London a century ago) rhymes with *tea*, and *a cup of tea* can be called *Rosie Lee*. *Apples and pears* rhymes with *stairs*, so *apples and pears* means *stairs*. The slang is still productive, for example *dog and bone* is now used for a (mobile) *phone*. Creating the rhyme is just the first stage—the next stage is to drop the rhyming part. Your *rosie* is your *cup of tea*, your *apples* your *stairs*, and your *dog* your *phone*. The system is intended to be complicated, and intended to exclude the outsider.

Some of the expressions have been around for long enough to acquire special meanings. *Hopping pot* means *lot*—a share or portion—but it has come to mean specifically a *bad lot* which someone is forced to accept. Required to take the blame for your colleague's mistakes? That's your hopping pot. Forced out of your job with minimal redundancy pay? That's also your hopping pot.

In the story, the hopping pot is a bad lot given to the son in his father's will—indeed it is his hopping pot. It is the genius of J. K. Rowling to take this well established phrase and transform it into a pot which hops, a pot which is a hopping pot both in terms of being a bad lot and in terms of being a one-legged pot that hops.

TO STIR something—as the old wizard does the contents of his hopping pot—is used in phrases like *to stir up your troubles*.

Someone who causes a stir causes aggravation and mischief. So, *don't stir it!* Yet we are told that the old wizard gives his pot a stir and rather than creating problems he solves them. There is something strange going on here. This isn't how we usually use the verb stir in English.

The solution seems to be in the idea of *Stir-up Sunday*, which in the Church of England is the last Sunday before Advent. In popular culture it is sometimes associated with the making of Christmas puddings, traditionally made about a month before Christmas. The idea of stirring up the Christmas pudding is what we all remember, though the term in fact comes from a text in the *Book of Common Prayer* designed to be read on this day:

> *Stir up, we beseech thee, O Lord, the wills of thy faithful people; that they, plenteously bringing forth the fruit of good works, may of thee be plenteously rewarded; through Jesus Christ our Lord, Amen.*

On Stir-up Sunday people are encouraged to do good works. The old wizard has taken to heart the message of Stir-up Sunday and spends his life doing good works. The young wizard is taught something of the message of Stir-up Sunday through the lesson of the Hopping Pot, though his reward seems to be no more than peace and quiet.

The noun phrase HOPPING POT is used in the following traditional song—reminding us that a hopping pot is a very real item.

Hopping Down Kent Way

Now hopping's just beginning,

We've got our time to spend.

We've only come down hopping,

To earn a quid if we can

With a tee-I-ay, tee-I-ay, tee-I-ee-I-ay.

Now early Monday morning,
The measurer he'll come round.
"Pick your hops all ready,
You'll pick them off the ground.:
With a tee-I-ay, tee-I-ay, tee-I-ee-I-ay.

Now early Tuesday morning,
The bookie he'll come round
With a bag of money,
He'll flop it on the ground.
Saying, "Do you want some money?"
"Yes sir if you please,
To buy a hock of bacon
And a roll of mouldy cheese."
With a tee-I-ay, tee-I-ay, tee-I-ee-I-ay.

They say all hopping's lousy,
I believe it's true.
Since I've been down hopping,
I've got a chat or two.
With a tee-I-ay, tee-I-ay, tee-I-ee-I-ay

Early Saturday morning.

It is our washing day.

We'll boil 'em in our hopping pot,

And we hang's 'em o'er the ground.

With a tee-I-ay, tee-I-ay, tee-I-ee-I-ay.

I say one, I say two,

No more hopping shall I do.

With a tee-I-ay, tee-I-ay, tee-I-ee-I-ay.

2. Exploring *The Fountain of Fair Fortune*

Stars ★★★★★★★ (7/7)

Pure genius! A remarkable and satisfying story which entertains as it teaches. A masterpiece!

Plot

The Fountain of Fair Fortune, found on a hill in an enchanted, walled garden, has the capacity to give fair fortune to the first person who bathes in it on Midsummer's Day. Before Midsummer sunrise many people—both Magic and Muggle—congregate outside the garden in the hope that they might be the one to bathe. Three witches meet there, discuss their problems, and motivated by pity one for the other they decide that they will try together to reach the fountain. Of the three witches, Asha is sick, Altheda is poor and Amata is broken-hearted.

At daybreak the three witches advance together, and creepers from the garden grab them and pull them in, along with Sir Luckless who has somehow got entangled with them. Only these four enter the enchanted garden, and begin their advance towards the Fountain. They meet three obstacles on their way, all of which Sir Luckless tries and fails to overcome, but which one of the three witches overcomes. The obstacles, along with the witch, the requirement and the solution, are as follows:

White Worm	Asha	Proof of Pain	Tears
Steep Slope	Altheda	Fruit of Labours	Sweat
Stream	Amata	Treasure of Past	Memories

Working together, the three witches and Sir Luckless make it to the summit of the hill and the edge of the Fountain of Fair Fortune. However Asha, exhausted by the climb, falls to the ground in pain and close to death. Altheda brews a potion from the herbs in the garden and water that Sir Luckless has in a gourd, and this potion cures Asha both of her immediate illness and her underlying sickness. She no longer needs to bathe. Altheda realises that her potion-making ability means that she has a source of income, and she too does not need to bathe. Amata comes to see that her lover had been faithless (presumably in contrast with the chivalry shown by Sir Luckless) and this cures her broken heart. She too no longer needs to bathe. By default Sir Luckless bathes, and emboldened by his good fortune asks Amata to marry him. She accepts—and they all live happily ever after.

CHARACTERS

Asha

Altheda

Amata

Sir Luckless

The White Worm

ILLUSTRATIONS

The shield of Sir Luckless is pictured with a serpent on it. In the Harry Potter books the serpent is associated with one of the Hogwarts founders, Salazar Slytherin. Now Sir Luckless is a Muggle and cannot be a descendant of Salazar Slytherin. He and Amata could just possibly be parents or perhaps more remote ancestors, a state of affairs which would make the pure-blood loving Salazar Slytherin a half-blood.

There is a lovely picture of the three witches and Sir Luckless. Sir Luckless is in the rear—indeed the picture emphasizes the leading role of the three women in this tale, even though it is Sir Luckless who has the first try at overcoming each obstacle. The environment is a pretty garden.

The Fountain of Fortune is pictured with its vertical support in the form of a dragon—a very long and very thin one. The head is visible at the top, two tiny wings at the side, and the scales of the whole body clearly drawn. Perhaps it is appropriate that the form of a magical creature should be used for the fountain.

THE PICTURE OF THE FOUNTAIN

The illustration showing the Fountain of Fair Fortune (on page 32 of the standard edition) includes a series of symbols. From top to bottom these seem to be:

(on the rim of the top basin) the astrological symbol for the planet Mars.

(on the top basin) the astrological symbols for the Moon and Sun combined.

(on the rim of the second basin) the astrological symbol for the planet Jupiter.

(on the second basin) The astrological symbol for the constellation Libra.

(on the rim of the third basin) The astrological symbol for the planet Mercury.

(on the third basin) The all-seeing eye—a talisman to ward off the evil eye.

(on the rim of the bottom basin) The astrological symbol of the planet Saturn.

(on the bottom basin). J. K. Rowling's symbol of the Deathly Hallows, as described in *Harry Potter and the Deathly Hallows*.

I don't think we should spend too long looking for the meaning behind these symbols. They are mostly astrological symbols. Just as the fountain has no special enchantment on it and Sir Luckless bathes in plain water, so these symbols have no special value. If anything J. K. Rowling is telling us that astrology is as much a fraud as the fountain.

ASSESSMENT

What a lovely story!

The story is regulated by its tidy plot. The events take place on one single day, between sunrise and sunset. The tableau is the fountain at the top of a hill and with the whole of the hill in a garden surrounded by a wall. The protagonists are three witches—a magic number, and a staple of fairy stories. The witches face three obstacles, and each witch uses a skill which she has to overcome that obstacle. There is also a "spare" in Sir Luckless who is caught up in the activity by chance. Sir Luckless tries to pass all three obstacles, but fails three times. He reaches the Fountain of Fair Fortune only because of his good fortune of being in the company of the three witches. They perceive him as chivalrous, and it is he who bathes.

The punch-line of this story cannot fail to grab our attention. The Fountain carries no enchantment, and the three witches and Sir Luckless have been "cured" without its magical intervention.

All the characters in this story behave well. They act with compassion for their companions, striving together for their common goal. The three witches know that only one of them can be successful, and have no plan for deciding who that one will be, yet nonetheless they co-operate successfully. When Sir Luckless joins them they know that the odds against success for each one of them have lengthened, yet they agree that he should go with them. When at the summit Asha falls ill there is no thought of one or all of them taking the final steps to the Fountain of Fair Fortune in order to win the race and themselves bathe. Rather they give thought to helping Asha to the Fountain (but cannot do this because are all are caring of their ill companion. Ultimately each one of the three witches gives up her chance to bathe of her own free will in the belief that one of her companions is the more needy.

Sir Luckless is the hardest character to assess. He is presented as an unheroic knight who is down on his luck. He seems to be of the type of Don Quixote, and his skeletally-thin horse seems to hint at this typology. It is easy to regard him as cowardly (which is perhaps his assessment of himself) though in fact he is the first to try to overcome each of the three obstacles that they face. His fortune in being the one who enters the fountain stands comparison with the fate of the cowardly lion in the *Wizard of Oz*, who is presented with a medal for courage and thereby becomes courageous. His dip in the fountain gives him self-confidence, and it is this sense of self worth that enables him to ask Amata to marry him. Throughout the story he is upstaged by the three witches, yet he is the winner of the quest for the Fountain of Fair Fortune.

In this story virtue is rewarded. This is immensely satisfying.

LITERARY PARALLELS

The concept of healing waters is commonplace, but the idea of water that heals only the first person to enter it is much rarer. The best known example is the pool of Bethesda in Jerusalem. John's Gospel tells us that the smooth water of the pool is sometimes disturbed when an angel comes down into the pool, and that at these times people believe that the first person to enter the water is cured. No proof is given that this belief is true, and it may be that the waters are just as unremarkable as those of the Fountain of Fair Fortune.

The idea of a fountain or spring at the top of a hill is indeed strange, yet many children will spot the nursery-rhyme parallel:

Jack and Jill went up a hill

To fetch a pail of water

Jack fell down and broke his crown

And Jill came tumbling after.

Leaving aside the unpleasant accident (crown here means forehead, so Jack fell and cut his forehead) we have two children going up a hill to a water source at the top of the hill.

It is perhaps easy to over-look, but the whole of the day-long action of this story takes place within a garden which is walled. This is a potent literary image for both the mediaeval and renaissance worlds. Outside the garden is the untamed wild; within is a human environment adapted for human needs. In Edmund Spenser's *The Faerie Queen* the garden is presented as *The Bower of Bliss*—the place where human comfort and delight is given full reign. Within The Fountain of Fair Fortune the garden must be huge, as it contains within it a hill which takes all day to climb, yet it remains a human environment. The obstacles within the garden are human made, and while they prevent progress they do not seem threatening. We hear that the garden grows health-giving herbs and has flowers within it. It is in all respects a wholesome and pleasant place.

LESSONS FOR LIFE

The shortest statement of the lesson of this tale is surely the tale itself. It is something to do with a realisation that happiness comes from within; that we need to change our outlook to be happy; that success comes to those who believe they can succeed; that virtue is rewarded.

ASHA is not established as an English first name though it is found in Eastern Europe (often spelt Asia). J. K. Rowling may intend it to relate to *ashes*. All three witches have names beginning with *a*, and perhaps this is all we should take from Asha.

ALTHEDA is a name once used in England, though almost unknown today. It means "healer," and is therefore appropriate for the character that is Altheda. It will be interesting to see if use of the name by J. K. Rowling in this story brings about a revival in its usage.

AMATA is related to the Latin verb to love, and reflects Amata's role in the story as deserted by her love.

The WHITE WORM brings to mind the book *The Lair of the White Worm* (1911) by Bram Stoker, best known for writing *Dracula*. Here the White Worm is modeled on the legendary Lambton Worm. Key to the image in both is a massive worm that stretches the whole way round a hill—in the case of the Lambton Worm ten times around the hill. THE LAMBTON WORM that seems to lie behind the White Worm of The Fountain of Fair Fortune is best known today from the North-East England traditional song. Sometimes it is written in the Geordie dialect of the Newcastle area, but in something resembling standard English it reads as follows. The Wear is a river and *bairns* are *children*.

One Sunday morning Lambton went

A-fishing in the Wear;

And catched a fish upon his hook

He thought looked very queer.

But whatt'n a kind of fish it was

Young Lambton couldn't tell-

He wasn't fash to carry it home,

So he hoyed it down a well

>*Chorus:*

>*Whisht! lads, haad yor gobs,*

>*An' aa'll tell ye aall an aaful story,*

>*Whisht! lads, haad yor gobs,*

>*An' Aa'll tel ye 'boot the worm.*

Now Lambton felt inclined to go

And fight in foreign wars.

He joined a troop of Knights that cared

For neither wounds nor scars,

And off he went to Palestine

Where queer things him befell,

An very soon forgot about

The queer worm i' the well.

But the worm got fat and growed and growed,

And growed an awful size;

He'd greet big teeth, a greet big gob,

An greet big goggle eyes.

An' when at nights he crawled about

To pick up bits of news,

If he felt dry upon the road,

He milked a dozen cows.

This fearful worm would often feed

On calves and lambs and sheep,

And swallow little bairns alive

When they laid down to sleep.

An when he'd eaten all he could

And he had had he's fill,

He crawled away an' lapped he's tail

Ten times round Penshaw Hill.

The news of this most awful worm

And his queer goings on

Soon crossed the seas, got to the ears

Of brave and bold Sir John.

So home he cam and catched the beast

And cut him in two halves,

And that soon stopped his eating bairns

And sheep and lambs and calves.

So now ye know how all the folks

On both sides of the Wear

Lost lots of sheep and lots of sleep

An lived in mortal fear.

So let's have one to brave Sir John

That kept the bairns from harm,

Saved coos an' calves by making halves

O' the famous Lambton Worm.

THE WONDERFUL WIZARD OF OZ appears to be a source for *The Fountain of Fair Fortune,* either conscious or subliminal. The book by L. Frank Baum (1900) has gone through countless editions, but it is through the 1939 film and later cinematic re-workings that most of us have become familiar with *The Wizard of Oz.* The characters in this story parallel those in the Fountain of Fair Fortune. *The Wizard of Oz* has one woman (Dorothy) leading three men (the Scarecrow, the Tin Woodman and the Cowardly Lion), while *The Fountain of Fair Fortune* has three women together leading one man. In *The Wizard of Oz* the gifts sought are a brain, a heart and courage—perhaps comparably abstract to the health, wealth and love sought by the three witches. The four meet obstacles on the way, go on a quest to defeat the Wicked Witch of the West, and ultimately are "cured" by the Wizard of Oz. He gives them useless articles, but such is their faith in him that he solves their problems without magic, just as does the Fountain of Fair Fortune.

3. EXPLORING *THE WARLOCK'S HAIRY HEART*

STARS ★ ★ ★ ★ (4/7)

This tale is a bloody and gruesome Gothic horror where virtue is punished, remorse is powerless and the moral of the tale is elusive. The tale's redeeming feature is that it presents the marvelously visual symbol of the Hairy Heart as a way of telling us that evil exists.

PLOT

A young warlock decides that he does not want to be made a fool by love, and using black magic cuts out his own heart. When his parents die he does not mourn them, and lives alone and untroubled. One day his pride is hurt when he overhears a comment that he is unable to find a wife, and decides that he would indeed marry. He finds a beautiful Maiden and courts her. She is flattered but feels his coldness, telling him at a banquet that she does not think he has a heart. The warlock shows her his heart, kept in a casket in a dungeon, now shrunken and covered in hair. The Maiden ask him to replace it in his chest. When he does this she embraces him. The language J. K. Rowling uses to describe his reaction is allusive, but she appears to suggest that he rapes her. He then rips out her heart which he means to use to replace his own Hairy Heart. However, he finds that he is unable to make the swap, and instead rips out his own heart, so dying.

CHARACTERS

The Warlock.

The Maiden.

Various "walk on" parts.

Illustrations

The tale contains a picture of the Hairy Heart. The arteries are neatly cut. Presumably J. K. Rowling got a sheep's heart from a butcher and drew it—adding some hairs. School children of J. K. Rowling's generation would have encountered on the school syllabus for Biology for twelve year olds the practical task of dissecting a heart—usually a sheep's heart—and drawing a labeled diagram of it.

There is also a picture of the dead Maiden and the Warlock in a pool of blood. It adds little to the story.

Assessment

On a technical note it has to be pointed out that there is a plot hole in this tale. The Warlock means to replace his own Hairy Heart with the Maiden's heart, but he is unable to do this because his Hairy Heart cannot be taken out of his chest. So because he will not be ruled by his heart he takes his heart out of his chest. This just doesn't add up—there is something wrong here.

Leaving aside the detail of its plot hole is the aspect that every reader must notice: this is a gruesome tale. We can be sure that Dumbledore's Beatrix Bloxam would not approve—and neither would our Beatrix Potter! Made into a film this story would struggle to get even an 18 Certificate, so graphic and extreme is the violence it describes. The fairy tale format has never shirked the shocking side of life, yet even within this genre *The Warlock's Hairy Heart* is extreme. A story such as this would not usually be written today for children, yet perhaps exposure to just such stories is a part of growing up.

In part we have stock characters. We have the tyrant, the man in authority, and the abused and persecuted Maiden. Fairy story parallels are not hard to find. Yet the resolution is supposed to be that the tyrant is cast low, or perhaps better mends his ways and becomes a good person, while the Maiden is supposed to come through her tribulations to triumph. This however is not the story of this tale.

In seeking to isolate himself from emotion, the Warlock is effectively distancing himself from society. He is not entering into relationships with people around him, either through marriage or through friendship. Throughout the early part of the story he is presented as harming no-one, and it would be possible to slip into the mistake of regarding his action as strange but not harmful. His sin of course is not in what he does, but in what he doesn't do—human beings are supposed to love.

An indication of his character is in the motif of the Hairy Heart itself. The Hairy Heart seems bestial, and the Warlock is therefore presented as less than human. By escaping human emotions he has lost something of his humanity, and ultimately he acts without reference to the moral values of humanity. The climax of the story presents a murder and a suicide, but both carried out with the maximum of brutality. The Warlock cuts open the Maiden's breast and rips out her heart, which he holds in his hand and licks and strokes. His own heart he himself cuts out, leaving us with the final image of the dying Warlock with a heart in each hand.

It is hard to escape the view that there is a sexual element in his attack and murder of the Maiden—that we are being told b Beedle (and therefore by J. K. Rowling) about a rape as well as a murder. The action is provoked by an embrace, and the response of the re-attached Hairy Heart is described in terms of the Warlock's "appetites" which are "powerful and perverse." Most telling is that the heart is licked and stroked by the Warlock. The theme is not developed—after all, this horrifically violent tale is being presented as a tale for children—yet there is I think quite enough hinted at for the adult readers to fill the gaps.

The Warlock is dehumanized in this story. He cannot love, and because of this perhaps isn't fully human. Ultimately his actions are evil, and perhaps he is therefore evil. There is a parallel with J. K. Rowling's development of the idea of the horcrux as a split soul created through the act of murder. Soul and heart are frequently almost synonyms, and here we have an act of violence against the owner's own heart which is just as evil as the violence against a soul involved in creating a horcrux. In the Harry Potter novels we are told that murder splits a soul. Possibly we should see murder as a part of the black art which enabled the Warlock to remove his own heart.

J. K. Rowling has an enormous fan base, plus an established reputation as a remarkable writer along with celebrity status. Probably she can get away with presenting a tale like this, yet anyone else would be hounded by the media and roundly condemned. This tale is too shocking, too distant from the spirit of safety which permeates our age. Probably J. K. Rowling should be seen as making something of a stand against excessive sheltering of children. Throughout the Harry Potter novels the children in the stories are not pampered, and probably this reflects her views. Life is as it is and the children all seem to cope with it, with some (limited) support and guidance from the teachers of Hogwarts and from Dumbledore, but largely through their own resilience and the help of their peer group. Ginny Weasley in *Harry Potter and the Chamber of Secrets* has a wretched year and ultimately is all but killed, and her reward from Dumbledore is an early night and a mug of hot chocolate. In writing this story J. K. Rowling is assuming a greater degree of resilience from her child readers than is generally assumed by our age. Many children will see the story as a comic horror and no more than this, and so be unscathed, but for those who do penetrate its deeper meaning it is a story which is little short of traumatic.

For in this story we have evil triumphant. There is no "and they all lived happily ever after." There is no sense of a greater good coming from the suffering of the protagonists. The Maiden has acted well in suggesting that the Warlock should reattach his heart, but dies a brutal death. Perhaps we should imagine that her reward comes in the next life (the sort of happy ending some have seen in the black despair of William Shakespeare's *King Lear*) though there is no hint of this in the tale. The Warlock has acted as a beast and dies through suicide. Just possibly we could see his action in ripping out his own heart as a realisation that the heart is not the heart he once had, and therefore not his, but again this is not actually said in the story. Rather we see an apparently evil man who kills the Maiden to steal her heart. All we truly learn from this tale is that evil exists.

What are we to do with the knowledge this tale gives? That evil exists in the world is a profound concept, but a necessary next step following this realisation is an understanding of how we intend to react to it. On this crucial topic the story is silent. Rather we have weak hints of possible courses of action in other areas, Are we to guard against locking away our own hearts? Is the decision not to love a sin? Perhaps, but the tale does explicitly not tell us. Rather it leaves us puzzled, and this must be its weakness.

LESSONS FOR LIFE

There is evil in the world. Horrible things happen. There is no justification for evil, no silver lining. This is a world in which Santa Claus does not exist, a world where there is no Fairy God-Mother to wave a wand and make everything right. The tale gives a brutal and despairing vision. Perhaps there is a warning—don't be like the Warlock, don't even be like the Maiden—therefore love, but love wisely. Perhaps some sort of response to the problem of evil as presented in this tale is offered by some of the other tales. But the response isn't here.

Language

The chief linguistic issue of this tale is with the word Warlock Curiously J. K. Rowling feels a need to explain it, and does so in a footnote to Dumbledore's comments. She comes up with the definition that a warlock is "one learned in dueling and all martial magic,", and suggests a Warlock is comparable to a Muggle knight.

This isn't what *warlock* means in English. Warlock can be a name for the devil, but is usually a name for someone in league with the devil and therefore possessing occult powers which they use for evil. This correct definition is completely at odds with the wrong definition that J. K. Rowling gives. Warlock is used in the Harry Potter books, including in the first one *Harry Potter and the Sorcerer's Stone*, where it is even a title that Dumbledore has. My theory is that J. K. Rowling made a mistake in originally using this totally inappropriate word because she did not understand what it meant, presumably seeing it as little more than a synonym for wizard. In the later Harry Potter books she appears to ditch it, suggesting that she has thought twice about it. Yet here in *The Tales of Beedle the Bard* it crops up again. Warlock is completely out of place in any children's book, be it this one, the Harry Potter novels or any other, and it is unacceptable that someone in league with the devil should be confused with the admirable Dumbledore. In *The Warlock's Hairy Heart* it is possible that the Warlock described really should be regarded as in league with the devil—he has certainly used black magic—and the name may in this case be justified as a correct use of an English word—correct in terms of the definition in the dictionary, rather than the wrong definition that J. K. Rowling invents.

The Warlock is described as having a "haughty mien." Such language is consciously archaizing, in that it is using the words of a past age. Most people today never use "mien," and even "haughty" has fallen out of fashion. "Mien" means the bearing or manner of a person, particularly as it expresses their character, so the idea is that the Warlock looks haughty because he really is haughty.

Amazingly HAIRY HEART really is a medical condition. Its proper name is *fibrinous pericarditis*—an inflammation of the heart which causes fibrous hairs to grow.

LYCANTHROPY, briefly mentioned in one of the footnotes, is again a real medical condition. Lycanthropy is a psychological condition where a patient imagines himself (or herself) to be a wolf or another animal, and may act as they imagine a wolf would act.

The manner by which the Warlock murders the Maiden and kills himself brings to mind the Viking BLOOD EAGLE. The Vikings who invaded the British Isles in the ninth to eleventh centuries have had a bad press, often undeserved. Yet in the practice of the Blood Eagle they exceed their own bloody reputation. Blood Eagle was a form of ritual slaughter of a defeated enemy as a sacrifice to the war god, Odin. An axe was use to cleave the chest cavity of the victim, and his heart pulled out. If done with sufficient speed—and the aim was speed—it was possible for the victim to see his own heart in the final moments of his life.

4. EXPLORING *BABBITTY RABBITTY AND HER CACKLING STUMP*

STARS ★★★ (3/7)

While it is an entertaining yarn this tale is ultimately over-complex and without a clear moral. If there is one of *The Tales of Beedle the Bard* that will be forgotten it will be this one.

PLOT

This is the most complex of the stories. The background is a Muggle King who decides that he alone should have magic powers. He therefore persecutes witches and wizards through a brigade of witch hunters, while at the same time seeking an instructor in magic. The person who takes this job is a charlatan, a Muggle with no magic ability, but someone who knows a few conjuring tricks and thus is able to deceive the King. The charlatan takes money from the King while providing him with a twig instead of a wand, and teaching him nonsense in lieu of magic. Babbitty Rabbity, who is a witch and the King's washerwoman, overhears the "lessons" and bursts out laughing. Feeling that he is being mocked, the King decides on a demonstration of his magic the next day, and will not accept the charlatan's objections—indeed he threatens to kill the charlatan. By chance at that time the charlatan sees Babbitty Rabbitty washing clothes by magic, and with the threat of denouncing her to the witch hunters he forces her to help him.

For the magic display Babbitty Rabbitty conceals herself in a bush and performs the spells supposedly performed by the King. These are as follows:

vanishing a lady's hat.

making a horse fly.

The King is then asked by the Captain to bring back to life the dog Sabre that has died through poisoning through eating a toadstool. As magic cannot raise the dead Babbitty Rabbitty cannot perform this task, though neither the King nor the charlatan know this.

The courtiers see the King's failure at this task and therefore doubt that the first two spells were genuine. The charlatan hits upon the idea of blaming the failure of an imaginary counter- spell on Babbitty Rabbitty, saying that a wicked witch is blocking the spells. She is revealed in the bush, and the Brigade of Witch Hunters chase her. We later realise (largely through Dumbledore's notes) that Babbitty Rabbitty is an animagus and can turn herself into a rabbit. This is what she does, and hides herself in a hole at the base of a tree. The Witch Hunters decide to cut down the tree, thinking that she has turned herself into a tree, but of course fail to harm Babbitty Rabbitty. Speaking from the hole at the base of what is now the stump she states that a witch or wizard cannot be killed by being cut in half, and that they should try the experiment on the charlatan, whom they believe to be a wizard. This they decide to do; the charlatan begs for mercy confessing that he is not a wizard, and is carried off to a dungeon. Speaking from the stump Babbitty Rabbitty makes the following demands to the King:

He should protect all witches and wizards in his Kingdom. If he doesn't he will feel on his own body all the pain inflicted on them.

He should set up a statue of Babbitty Rabbitty upon the tree stump to remind him of his foolishness.

The King agrees, and Babbitty Rabbitty waits until the coast is clear and hops away. The King does as he has promised. And we do just about get to "and they all lived happily ever after."

CHARACTERS

King

Charlatan

Babbitty Rabbitty

Captain of Witch Hunters

The Brigade of Witch Hunters

Sabre

ILLUSTRATIONS

The story includes a whole-page illustration of a horse magically thrown up into the air. It is not a very good picture. Pity the poor horse here—I hope there was a happy landing! The picture does perhaps make the point that a horse thrown into the air would be an impressive piece of magic, and, even with the subsequent failure to bring back to life the dead dog, the courtiers should be impressed by the performance.

The picture that J. K. Rowling does not give us is of the lady's vanished hat. At least I can't find it!

ASSESSMENT

This is not a tidy story. The plot is very complex for a fairy story, and surprisingly hard to remember. The length of the plot summary above hints at the many steps and the amount of detail which is needed just to give a coherent plot. There is no clear pattern or structure within it. Instead the story seems almost to have disconnected sections. There is significant scene setting in the form of information about the persecution of the witches and wizards by the Brigade of Witch Hunters which is almost a story in itself. Then there is the King's foolishness in believing that he can learn magic, along with the exploitation of his foolishness by the charlatan.

Subsequently we have the day of the demonstration, and finally Babbitty Rabbitty's deception as the Cackling Stump. All these areas are stories in their own right.

There is a hint of character depth in all three of the main characters, which might go against the fairy tale conventions. Thus the King is foolish, yet wants to learn. He seeks to be worthy as his teacher directs, and it is his misfortune that his teacher is a charlatan. Ultimately the King accepts the teaching of Babbitty Rabbitty, and he does perhaps develop into a less foolish King as a consequence. The charlatan is the archetype of the confidence trickster, yet in the end he makes a confession of what he has done, which might be a first step towards some redemption in another tale. Babbitty Rabbitty lives on her wits. While we tend to approve her actions she is nonetheless taking part in a deception, which really isn't very nice. She resolves this simply be leaving— Dumbledore's notes suggest that she crossed the English Channel from France to England in her cauldron.

At the end of the story we do have a gain in that the persecution of Witches and Wizards stops. This however is scarcely convincing, for if it were that easy to frighten the foolish King some other Witch or Wizard would have done it long before. The statue of Babbitty Rabbitty—in gold no-less—may indeed remind the King of his foolishness, and may symbolize real learning.

The key concept of the story is that death is an absolute. Magic cannot raise the dead. Vanishing hats and flying horses are possible, at least in the Magic world—but for the Magic world as for ours the dead cannot be raised.

Lessons for Life

Don't try to find lessons for life in tales such as this one. Not everything has a moral, not every fairy story teaches us something. This one probably doesn't have a moral and doesn't teach us anything very much. Enjoy as an entertaining story—then forget it.

Language

The name Babbitty Rabbitty is an example of motherese—the sort of reduplicative language that mothers sometimes use when speaking to young children—think *bow-wow*, or *choo-choo* or *moo-cow*. Babbitty of course is able to change into a rabbit, and it is this ability which gives her what is virtually a surname, modified to reduplicate the sound of her first name. If we are to see a real person behind the character in the tale then her name was perhaps Babbitty The ending –itty looks like a diminutive, making a nickname, suggesting that the name is really something like Baba.

To CACKLE originally meant to make a noise like a goose. It has come to mean to laugh with a noise like a goose, and has become a critical word to describe some laughter, particularly mocking laughter. In many stories witches are said to cackle. Babbitty Rabbitty indeed cackles from the hole beneath the tree stump, but this is not central to the plot of the story and it is surprising that it should make it to the title of the story.

BABBITTY brings to mind the witch BABA YAGA. The idea of a witch travelling in a cauldron is not found in the Harry Potter books. It is however a staple of Slavonic mythology, where the witch BABA YAGA travels in a giant pestle, effectively a cauldron, paddled across the sky with a mortar. Baba Yaga is a complex character, certainly more than just a wicked witch though there is something of this too in some stories about her. She lives in a hut without windows or door (she enters and leaves through the chimney) which is raised above the ground on giant chickens' legs.

The story of Baba Yaga has been popularized in Western Europe and in America through the work of composer Modest Mussorgsky, who presents her as one of his *Pictures at an Exhibition*.

WITCH-HUNTING was authorized by Pope Innocent VIII in 1484 through the issue of the papal bull known by its opening words *Summis desiderantes affectibus* (Desiring with supreme ardor) which gave a Dominican Inquisitor Heinrich Kramer explicit authority to persecute supposed witches. In the world of Babbitty Rabbitty and her Cackling Stump witches do exist, and the persecution is against a group of people because of a difference, so it is racism. In our world of courses witches in the sense envisaged do not exist, and the Pope's authorized persecution was against ordinary people no different from their neighbors.

5. Exploring *The Tale of the Three Brothers*

Stars ★★★★★★★ (7/7)

Superb! This story needs thinking about, and it repays thought. In good moral fable tradition this tale has something important to teach us.

Plot

Three brothers on a journey find that they must cross a dangerous river where many travelers have died. Being wizards they conjure a bridge so that they can cross safely. On the bridge they meet Death, who had expected to tale their lives as the crossed the river. He provides them with three gifts:

A wand made of elder wood, more powerful than any other.

A stone with the power to bring back the dead.

A cloak of invisibility to hide from Death.

The first brother uses the wand to kill an enemy, boasts of the wand, and has his throat cut while he sleeps and so dies. The second brother uses the stone to bring back a ghost of a woman he loves. She does not want to be back in the world, and he kills himself to be with her. Death therefore claims two of his three victims. The third brother leads a long life hidden by the cloak, and when it is time to die removes the cloak and greets Death as an old friend.

Characters

The three brothers are not named in the story itself, but in *Harry Potter and the Deathly Hallows* we are told what Xenophilius Lovegood believes to be their names. These are:

Antioch Peverell.

Cadmus Peverell.

Ignotus Peverell.

Death is presented as a character. This is in keeping with the mediaeval presentation of Death personified as the Grim Reaper.

There are several "walk on parts", including the nameless wizard who kills the first brother, and the women whose shade is brought back from the dead by the second brother.

Illustrations

We do have an illustration of the Deathly Hallows, plus a skull. It is necessary to know what the Deathly Hallows are in order to interpret the picture; the skull of course represents death. The picture itself isn't very helpful.

We also have a picture of the grave of one of the Peverell brothers, complete with symbols. In the centre is J. K. Rowling's symbol of the Deathly Hallows combining the wand, the stone and the cloak. On either side a coffin and crossed bones are *memento mori*—something designed to remind us all that we will die. While the coffin used in this way seems to be a J. K. Rowling touch, the crossed bones are familiar in old church memorials and on churchyard gravestones. The earliest use of crossed bones is associated with the Knights Templar; more recently they have been used by individuals as well as by groups including the Freemasons. Death lurks behind the grave stone, with his bony fingers visible at each side. The skull of Death above the stone is winged, signifying his fast arrival.

ASSESSMENT

This is a great story.

The meeting with Death on the bridge should surely be interpreted as a brush with death. Some time in their youth the three brothers had a close shave with death, and it affected them profoundly. The elder brother lived a life of violence, and died young through violence. The response of the second brother is to want to join the dead, and he kills himself. The third lives a long life, and when finally death comes he accepts it. The story encourages us to emulate the third brother. In the iconography of the story it is better to remain hidden under the cloak than to use unbeatable wands or resurrection stones.

An extended assessment of this tale is given in *Harry Potter and the Deathly Hallows* by the character Xenophilius Lovegood. Probably we are to regard him as too credulous, too ready to believe the story, yet nothing that he suggests in his commentary on the tale is disproved in that book.

Lovegood stresses that the three objects given by Death are real objects:

The Elder Wand indeed seems to appear in the history of the Harry Potter world—though with many different names.

The Resurrection Stone appears lost, though Lovegood has no problem with the idea that it might exist. He challenges Hermione to prove that it doesn't exist.

The Invisibility Cloak is a plot device in every one of the Harry Potter novels.

Lovegood suggests that the three gifts of Death should be seen together as what he describes as the Deathly Hallows. He believes that the person who unites the three would be "master" of Death.

In Harry Potter and the Deathly Hallows it is of course Harry Potter who unites the three objects:

The Invisibility Cloak he inherits from his father James Potter. The assumption is that James Potter is a descendant of Ignotus Peverell. We hear in the tale that Ignotus leaves the cloak to his son, and presumably we are to imagine a succession of parents given the cloak to their children, and the cloak passing in secrecy through the generations.

The Resurrection Stone has been made into a ring and at some time become an heirloom of Salazar Slytherin. Ultimately it passes to the Gaunt family, and is sold by Voldemort's mother. Voldemort steals it and murders its owner, and makes it into a horcrux. Dumbledore tracks it down, and passes it to Harry in his will hidden in a snitch.

The Elder Wand is the wand of Dumbledore, the wand buried with him, and which Voldemort steals from his grave.

The Deathly Hallows are united only once, and only for a brief time. When, during the battle of Hogwarts, Harry walks into the Forbidden Forest to meet Voldemort he has the Invisibility Cloak in a pocket. Because he is near his death the snitch Dumbledore has given him opens, and he has the Resurrection Stone in his hand. The Elder Wand is in Voldemort's hand and Harry does not touch, yet it is his. Shortly before Dumbledore's death the wand transfers its allegiance to Draco Malfoy (who disarms him) and subsequently to Harry (who disarms Draco). So although the Elder Wand is held by Voldemort it belongs to Harry. At the time when the Deathly Hallows are united in Harry, Voldemort kills Harry.

Except he doesn't kill him, at least not quite. Rather Harry has a near-death experience, where he believes he is speaking with Dumbledore on Kings Cross Station. He has a choice, either to board a train and go on (to die) or to go back to his life and defeat Voldemort. Harry is truly "master" of Death in that it is his choice whether to live or to die.

The fate of the Deathly Hallows is set out:

The Elder Wand is returned to Dumbledore's grave. We may assume that sooner or later someone will dig it up again.

The Resurrection Stone has been dropped on the forest floor, and Harry makes no effort to find it. Presumably sooner or later this magical object will re-surface.

Harry keeps the Invisibility Cloak, and will presumably give it to one of his sons.

In *Harry Potter and the Deathly Hallows* are several references to a rune-like symbol representing the three magical gifts Death gave the three brothers. The elder wand is represented by a vertical line, the resurrection stone by a circle, and the invisibility cloak by a triangle. Any reader may draw this symbol from the instructions given in the clear description of Xenophilius Lovegood. My drawing from his description is:

The symbol produced is far more than an invention of J. K. Rowling. Rather it is a staple of Western art and iconography, with early forms found in both Germanic and Celtic tradition. Consciously or subconsciously, J. K. Rowling is tapping into this tradition.

One interpretation of the symbol is that it represents simply humanity. The triangle is a long-established symbol for man, the circle an equally old symbol for woman. The vertical line suggests a division, here a division between male and female. Combined in this symbol we have male and female together, all humanity.

Yet there is another interpretation that surely J. K. Rowling who took the trouble to describe this symbol must be aware of—it is a fundamental Christian symbol. The equilateral triangle is the most basic symbol of the Trinity, of the Father, the Son and the Holy Ghost. The circle, the infinite shape without an end, is the most basic symbol of God, eternal and uncreated. The concept of the three and the one united is in all the Creeds of the Christian Church, but is most clearly set out in the Athanasian Creed:

> *We worship one God in trinity and the Trinity in unity, neither confusing the persons nor dividing the divine being. For the Father is one person, the Son is another, and the Spirit is still another. But the deity of the Father, Son, and Holy Spirit is one, equal in glory, coeternal in majesty.*

In the mediaeval world the shape J. K. Rowling describes was called the Coat of Arms of God. There is an echo of this concept in *Harry Potter and the Deathly Hallows*—think of the discussion where the symbol of the Hallows inscribed on the stone in Marvolo's ring is also described as a coat of arms. To the mediaeval mind the symbol perfectly shows the three persons of God, with the three points being God the Father, God the Son, God the Holy Spirit. Many mediaeval presentations were annotated with words to make this point even clearer. On the sides of the triangle are found the words "is not." The Father is not the Son; the Son is not the

Holy Spirit; the Holy Spirit is not the Father. The three persons of the Holy Trinity are perceived as separate and must not be confused, for they are not one. Yet the mediaeval annotation places in the central circle the name God and states God is the Father; God is the Son; God is the Holy Spirit. Within each of the three separate persons of the Trinity is God, yet each person is distinct. The symbol of the Coat of Arms of God is fundamental to the mediaeval idea of Christianity in that it reduces to a simple diagram the abstruse reasoning around the concept of the Trinity.

The vertical line in the symbol of the Deathly Hallows may be interpreted as the Christian cross. The top of the circle provides the horizontal cross-piece of the cross. An interpretation is that through the cross the trinity defeats death. In *Harry Potter and the Deathly Hallows* the possessor of all three Hallows is seen as master of Death.

LITERARY PARALLELS

J. K. Rowling presents a possible parallel with *The Pardoner's Tale*, one of Geoffrey Chaucer's *Canterbury Tales*. There is a parallel of sorts, but it is not close.

In *The Pardoner's Tale* we are told the story of three revelers who are drinking in a tavern in a town where many have been killed by the plague. While they are rather merry from the drink they hear a bell toll for a funeral, and they make the boast that they will go and find Death and kill him. Out they go, and meet with a very old man, who they treat very rudely. The man says he is old and wants to die, but cannot. In answer to their question he says he knows where Death is, and directs them to a tree nearby. Beneath the tree the three revelers find not Death but a big pile of treasure. They forget all about their quest and think instead about how they will carry the treasure away. One of the revelers is sent back to town to get a wheelbarrow and something for them all to drink, while the other two keep guard. While waiting they decide to kill the third when he returns, as divided between just two they will have a bigger share than divided between three. The reveler who has gone to town gets the wheelbarrow and the drinks, but poisons the drinks with rat-poison, planning to kill his fellows and keep all the treasure for himself. He returns to his friends, and is promptly murdered by them. Then they drink the poisoned drink and die. The three revelers therefore succeed in their quest and find Death.

This tale is regarded as one of the great short-stories in the English language. It provokes a lot of thought. Is it arrogant to think we can defeat Death? Can we find Death? Does wealth corrupt? Does wealth lead to Death? There are also questions around the character of the old man. Chaucer appears to have presented a mediaeval legend, that of the Wandering Jew. The story is that the Wandering Jew is Judas Iscariot who betrayed Jesus, and who is punished by being unable to die. He spends his life as an old man wandering the world, tapping on the ground with his stick as if to say "open up and let me in." In the same story Chaucer manages to present Death both as a force which kills indiscriminately through the plague and through murder, and as a force to be desired as the natural end of life.

LESSONS FOR LIFE

In *The Tale of the Three Brothers* we have three different responses to Death.

The first of these is symbolized by the Elder Wand, and may represent the vanity of power and authority. By having a wand that cannot be defeated in a duel, the elder brother has the tool that will bring him power and wealth and authority, and which he hopes will enable him to defeat Death. His possession of such a wand will bring violence and treachery, and in the terms of the story it will also bring Death. Such an unbeatable wand will always be associated with blood and destruction. Dumbledore who owns the wand keeps its true identity secret. He owns it without seeming to come to harm from it, but it is far from clear that it does him any good either, and he might as well have used instead an ordinary wand. In trying to pass it to Severus Snape he is leaving a dubious bequest, particularly in view of Snape's previously checkered history, and it is perhaps fortunate that his plan is frustrated. Snape armed with such a wand would have been a formidable ally—or a formidable opponent.

The second response is that of the middle brother who tries with the Resurrection Stone to bring the dead back. Of course he cannot do this, though he can raise an unwilling shade who does not want to be back from beyond the veil. The second brother's response to Death is that of a necromancer, and ultimately he finds that his dabbling in such doubtful arts is unsatisfactory. He kills himself. The tale does not develop this aspect, yet what we are told about is a suicide, an attempt to die when the brother decides, not when Death decides.

The response of the third brother is to hide from Death while he may. He lives a full and happy life, and when he comes to die he greets Death as an old friend. The tale goes out of its way to say that he took off the cloak, which suggests a degree of volition in accepting that Death will find him.

LANGUAGE

The Tale of Beedle the Bard does not call the three gifts of Death *Hallows*, though *Harry Potter and the Deathly Hallows* of course does. *Hallow* is not a word in the English language—at least it wasn't until J. K. Rowling made it a word. The closest approach is *hallowed* in the Lord's Prayer—*hallowed be Thy name*—where hallowed means something like blessed.

The sense that J. K. Rowling gives to Hallows is something made sacred by death, or perhaps something which encapsulates within it a response to death. The concept of uniting the Hallows may therefore symbolize a comprehensive response to the challenge of death.

The names of the three brothers—Antioch, Cadmus and Ignotus—are given in *Harry Potter and the Deathly Hallows*, though not in the *The Tale of Beedle the Bard* or in Dumbledore's notes.

ANTIOCH was once a major city of the Roman Empire. It is the city where the word *Christian* was first used to describe a follower of Jesus Christ, and one of the four ancient Christian cities— Jerusalem, Alexandria, Antioch and Rome. Now a town in eastern Turkey close to the Syrian border with the name Antakya, Antioch is remembered in the West for its Christian associations. It is surely this heritage which inspired J. K. Rowling's name for one of the brothers.

CADMUS is a Greek prince from the mists of time, described by the Greek historian Herodotus as living about 2000BC. He is remembered both as the founder of the Greek city of Thebes, and as the man who introduced the alphabet to the Greek language.

IGNOTUS is not usually used as a name. It is the Latin word for unknown, and reflects his role as the brother who hid from death, remaining unknown until he chose to take of the cloak.

PEVERELL—the surname of the brothers—may relate to Julian Peveril, the hero of Sir Walter Scott's novel *Peveril of the Peak* (1822). Walter Scott is a master teller of stories from the history of Scotland and England, and Peveril embodies many of the heroic ideals of both Kingdoms.

J. K. Rowling has given us powerful and historic names as the names of the three brothers.

6. Exploring Dumbledore's Notes

Stars ★★★★ (4/7)

For Harry Potter fans these notes are nice to read, and at times they are funny. However they are open to the charge that they are little more than a filler, designed to bulk up five short stories to something which is book length.

Albus Dumbledore or J. K. Rowling?

We are asked to believe that the critical notes on the tales are by Albus Dumbledore. Yet in reality the voice is that of J. K. Rowling, and in these notes we are given a glimpse of her views and her thinking.

Bearing in mind the length of the five tales there is by comparison a lot of these notes. In the standard edition, while the book runs to 125 pages (17 pages of front-matter and 108 pages of book proper) just 54 pages are taken up by the tales themselves. Basically half of the book is Dumbledore's notes. Most readers would have preferred more tales and less notes, or even more tales and no notes at all. Yet the notes do make us smile, and do perhaps give us a glimpse at how J. K. Rowling thinks.

6.1 Exploring Dumbledore's Notes on *The Wizard and the Hopping Pot*

Dumbledore glosses the tale giving it a meaning it needs were it to work properly, but which is in fact a meaning that the tale does not have. He states that the young wizard's "conscience awakes", which should of course be the point of the story, but this moral just isn't there as the tale stands. He then goes on to express surprise that the tale has survived at all, given that its sentiments were at odds with the spirit of the age. Somehow on the same page he manages to call his reader a "nincompoop."

The nincompoop is of course Dumbledore (or is it J. K. Rowling?)—a point he is probably big-hearted enough to accept. Many fairy stories in England are around the legend of King Arthur—yet King Arthur was the enemy who fought against the English, and we might find it surprising that the English have preserved fairy stories which treat him as the hero. The point is that fairy stories live or die according to their own strengths and weaknesses, not according to social factors.

Dumbledore draws our attention to the issue of racism and the implicit condemnation of racism made by the tale. Clearly this is a theme for the twenty-first century world, for however much progress has been made in race relations in Britain and North America we can be sure that more needs to be done. He also presents a sugar-coated version of the same tale, which Dumbledore quite rightly points out is not what children want.

BEATRIX BLOXAM the author of *Toadstool Tales* brings to mind BEATRIX POTTER (1866-1943). Miss Potter (as she is often called, rather like Mrs Bloxam) was a specialist in the academic description of toadstools before turning almost by chance to writing tales for children. Her *Tale of Peter Rabbit* and *Tale of Squirrel Nutkin* started a series of more than two dozen sweet, innocent and pretty tales, presumably enjoyed by children in her day though it is almost unthinkable that a child of our age could like them. Dumbledore is not a fan of Beatrix Bloxam, and we can reasonably infer that J. K. Rowling is similarly not a fan of Beatrix Potter.

6.2 EXPLORING DUMBLEDORE'S NOTES ON *THE FOUNTAIN OF FAIR FORTUNE*

Dumbledore draws our attention to the marriage at the end of the tale, which is between a Witch and a Muggle. In the Harry Potter books this is seen as comparable to a mixed-race marriage, and the idea therefore raises issues of prejudice and racism. Again the emphasis is on the theme of racism. Certainly it is present, both in this and two other of the tales, but Dumbledore's focus on this theme seems surprising. It would be interesting to know where and when in her life J. K. Rowling has personally encountered the issue of racism. The locations in Britain associated with J. K. Rowling (Bristol/Gloucestershire/Forest of Dean; Exeter/Devonshire; Edinburgh) are not locations particularly associated with problems of racism, though of course problems may happen anywhere.

Dumbledore also points out that this tale is one of the most popular. Seemingly J. K. Rowling has recognised the qualities of her own tale. Arguably this is the best.

We have a humorous interlude in Dumbledore's description of the staging of a dramatized version of the tale at Hogwarts. The story he tells could be summarized by the phrase "if it can go wrong, it will go wrong":

Amata and Sir Luckless have a real-life falling out.

The White Worm explodes.

A fire breaks out.

Asha and Amata have a real-life fight (over Sir Luckless).

Professor Beery was injured.

Many students went to the hospital wing.

The Great Hall smelt of wood smoke for several months.

The inevitable result is that Hogwarts decides not to stage a play again—a solution which might appeal to the teachers at many real-life schools!

Plays do not feature in the Harry Potter books, and it may be that the world J. K. Rowling has created is envisaged without its great playwrights.. The concept of making a play out of a fable is how drama started in the English speaking world in the age before Shakespeare. Stories just like *The Fountain of Fair Fortune*, short and with a tiny cast of actors, were presented for the education of viewers. These Miracle and Morality Plays were once well-known and well-loved in every town in England. The best known is *The Moral Play of Everyman*, which gives the flavor of a Fountain of Fair Fortune adapted for the stage.

Through the humor of Lucius Malfoy's letter to Dumbledore demanding the removal of this tale from the library at Hogwarts, J. K. Rowling introduces the topic of banned books. This issue has a mediaeval flavor, yet it is a part of our world still. The biggest ban on books is provided by the *Index liborum prohibitorum* (list of prohibited books) of the Roman Catholic church. The Index contains such English classics as John Milton's *Paradise Lost*— indeed when I lectured on this book at a British university I had a Roman Catholic student who prioritized his church over his grades and refused to read it (I found him an alternative to study). Dan Brown's best-seller *The Da Vinci Code* is also on the *Index* and was condemned from the pulpit by Roman Catholic priests. Sales of this book soared in the week following the Sunday sermons that condemned it. The Islamic faith has its own prohibitions—the best known is probably the ban on Salman Rushdie's *Satanic Verses*. Cultural sensibilities have led to cultural bans—the effective prohibition of carols being played in shops in Britain is arguably a form of censorship. Some American schools have banned the Harry Potter books, on the grounds that they are about witches and wizards and are therefore asserted to be satanic. The argument does not hold water—magic in the Harry Potter books is an alternative technology akin to that in science fiction, not a result of communing with the devil through black magic—but that does not stop some schools banning the books. Presumably some American schools will ban *The Tales of Beedle the Bard* as the result of a letter written by some real-life Lucius Malfoy.

THE MORAL TALE OF EVERYMAN dates from the late fifteenth century (very much the time associated with Beedle the Bard) and was popular for around a century. The story is that God sends Death to bring Everyman (that's you and me) to judgment. Everyman seeks a companion for the journey, and finds that the only friend who will go with him is his good deeds.

HERE BEGINETH A TREATISE HOW THE HIGH FATHER OF HEAVEN SENDETH DEATH TO SUMMON EVERY CREATURE TO COME AND GIVE ACCOUNT OF THEIR LIVES IN THIS WORLD AND IS IN MANNER OF A MORAL PLAY.

Messenger: I pray you all give your audience,

And here this matter with reverence,

By figure a moral play-

The Summoning of Everyman called it is,

That of our lives and ending shows

How transitory we be all day.

This matter is wondrous precious,

But the intent of it is more gracious,

And sweet to bear away.

The story saith—Man, in the beginning,

Look well, and take good heed to the ending,

Be you never so gay!

Ye think sin in the beginning full sweet,

Which in the end causeth thy soul to weep,

When the body lieth in clay.

Here shall you see how Fellowship and Jollity,

Both Strength, Pleasure, and Beauty,

Will fade from thee as flower in May.

For ye shall here, how our heavenly King

Calleth Everyman to a general reckoning:

Give audience, and here what he doth say.

6.3 Exploring Dumbledore's Notes on *The Warlock's Hairy Heart*

This story may well cause children to have nightmares, as Dumbledore imagines. One hopes that parents read stories like this themselves before reading them to their little children as a bedtime story.

Dumbledore tells us that this story is about a quest for invulnerability, where the Warlock is seeking to escape the buffeting of human emotion. His analysis is surely correct. He then launches into a discussion which equates the Warlock's splitting of heart from body with the idea of a horcrux—the concept of a split soul that is a plot theme of the final two Harry Potter novels. The idea of course appeals to Potter fans as it is a link between the world of Beedle and the world we see in the novels.

Throughout the Harry Potter novels, Dumbledore speaks of love and of death. The two strands are drawn together in one of the two quotations which are found at the start of *Harry Potter and the Deathly Hallows,* from the Quaker writer William Penn. Loving—having a heart—is a necessary preparation for the acceptance of death. Because the Warlock cannot love he cannot prepare for death, and his death is therefore all the more shocking.

WILLIAM PENN's writing on death in *More Fruits of Solitude* is often presented as a poem. Part of it is used at the start of *Harry Potter and the Deathly Hallow.* Penn's words are reflected the thinking we associate with Dumbledore, and ideas which run throughout the Harry Potter books.

And this is the Comfort of the Good,

that the Grave cannot hold them,

and that they live as soon as they die.

For Death is no more than a Turning of us over

from Time to Eternity.

Nor can there be a Revolution without it;

for it supposes the Dissolution of one form,

in order to the Succession of another.

Death then, being the Way and Condition of Life,

we cannot love to live,

if we cannot bear to die.

They that love beyond the World,

cannot be separated by it.

Death cannot kill, what never dies.

Nor can Spirits ever be divided

that love and live in the same Divine Principle;

the Root and Record of their Friendship.

If Absence be not death, neither is theirs.

Death is but Crossing the World,

as Friends do the Seas;

They live in one another still.

For they must needs be present,

that love and live in that which is Omnipresent.

In this Divine Glass,

they see Face to Face;

and their Converse is Free, as well as Pure.

This is the Comfort of Friends,

that though they may be said to Die,

yet their Friendship and Society are, in the best Sense,

ever present, because Immortal.

6.4 EXPLORING DUMBLEDORE'S NOTES ON *BABBITTY RABBITTY AND HER CACKLING STUMP*

Dumbledore draws our attention to what J. K. Rowling presumably regards as the central message of this tale—that magic cannot bring back the dead. Death is absolute. Dumbledore explores this idea with reference to an imagined wizard philosopher, one Bertrand de Pensées-Profondes (Bertrand of the Deep Thoughts). In our world the idea might be explored with reference to real philosophers or the advances of medicine. We have indeed pushed at the boundaries of death. A stopped heart may be restarted and a person may in this sense seem to come back from the dead. Yet death remains an absolute.

His comments on animagi extend the imaginary world of J. K. Rowling somewhat, though there is little here that is new to keen readers of the Harry Potter novels.

Harry Potter fans will find some interest in these notes, though anyone else may possibly regard them as the least interesting seven pages penned by J. K. Rowling.

BERTRAND RUSSELL (1872-1970) is the philosopher who seems implied by the name Bertrand de Pensées-Profondes. Russell has made an outstanding contribution to twentieth century philosophy and mathematics. His personal beliefs led to him campaigning for votes for women, while his pacifism caused his imprisonment during the First World War. He has shaped thinking on a great range of topics, including responses to racism and the ethics of sexuality. As a champion of humanitarian ideals and freedom of thought he has had an enormous influence on our world.

PENSÉES is the name of the best known work by the French philosopher and mathematician Blaise Pascal (1623-1662).

6.5 EXPLORING DUMBLEDORE'S NOTES ON *THE TALE OF THE THREE BROTHERS*

Dumbledore points the irony of the legend he says has grown up around the Deathly Hallows, the very legend that in *Harry Potter and the Deathly Hallows* motivates Xenophilius Lovegood. For while the tale stresses that Death cannot be mastered, the legend states exactly the opposite, that the owner of all three Hallows can master Death.

There is humor in Dumbledore's views of the real existence of the Deathly Hallows. With our knowledge of the Harry Potter books we can deduce the following:

At the time of writing Dumbledore owned the Elder Wand, and he knew that it was indeed the Elder Wand. He had the good sense to keep quiet about it.

At the time of writing Dumbledore had looked after the Invisibility Cloak for ten years, and had examined it thoroughly. It is indeed a perfect invisibility cloak, and does indeed seem to be one of the Hallows, though this is never proved.

At the time of writing Dumbledore does not have the Resurrection Stone—rather he acquires it a few months later. When he finds it he recognizes it for what it is, which suggests he does indeed believe in its existence.

His comments about these three objects are therefore fascinating, as he conveys the wrong impression without actually lying:

Claims that they own an unbeatable wand have been made by a succession of wizards who subsequently are beaten. True!

He says no-one has claimed to have found the Invisibility Cloak. True!

The stone has not been found. In fact Dumbledore knows that Voldemort recently owned it, and it has only recently been lost. True!

Dumbledore is dismissive of the story of the Deathly Hallows, which he clearly knows exist. It is as if he is deliberately throwing people off the scent, so that the Deathly Hallows will remain hidden. He has kept quiet about his wand, and he wants to safeguard Harry by keeping the cloak hidden. When (as we are told in *Harry Potter and the Half Blood Prince*) he finds the Resurrection Stone his first thought is to use it himself, and he would presumably have wanted to keep this quiet also. In rejecting the concept of the Deathly Hallows, Dumbledore quotes "Hope springs eternal,", which is half a line from the poem *An Essay on Man* (1733-34) by Alexander Pope. The poem expresses themes that Dumbledore himself expounds:

Hope humbly then; with trembling pinions soar;

Wait the great teacher Death, and God adore.

What future bliss He gives not thee to know,

But gives that hope to be thy blessing now.

Hope springs eternal in the human breast:

Man never is, but always to be, blest.

The soul, uneasy and confin'd from home,

Rests and expatiates in a life to come.

Here Death is seen not as the Grim Reaper but rather the Great Teacher. We must wait for Death—not taunt him as the first brother does, or kill ourselves as does the second, but simply wait for Death who is seen as a friend who comes to take our soul home. The third brother at the end of his life greets Death as a friend, as we all should do.

EGBERT is the name of several prominent Anglo-Saxons, though may perhaps be identified with Egbert King of Kent (664-63) who ruled one of the seven English Kingdoms which existed before they came together in England. This Egbert was a violent man who is believed to have killed his two cousins Aethelred and Aethelberht, son of his uncle Eormenred. Eormenred may be equated with the EMERIC mentioned by Dumbledore.

The inspiration for GODELOT is something of a puzzle, but HEREWARD THE WAKE is a part of English history, folklore and literature. Hereward was the leader of the resistance to William the Conqueror, a very real figure who was killed in 1072, along with thousands of soldiers and civilians slaughtered in William the Conqueror's brutal subjugation of the Midlands and North of England. In folklore Hereward is treated with King Alfred and Robin Hood as popular heroes fighting for the freedoms of the English. Today Hereward is the nickname and motto of Number 2 Squadron Royal Air Force.

The name BARNABAS DEVERILL may possibly be interpreted simply through the similarity of Deverill and devil—this man is simply an evil Dark Wizard. In England "The Deverills" are a group of villages on the edge of Salisbury Plain (of Stonehenge fame, and therefore with magical associations). The four villages are Longbridge Deverill, Brixton Deverill, Monkton Deverill and Kingston Deverill. The name crops up in P. G. Wodehouse's Jeeves and Wooster stories in the form Deverill Hall, so not all uses are sinister.

LOXIAS is a name for the god Apollo, particularly used in the name Oracle of Loxias. This shrine was destroyed by Cadmus, the name of one of the three brothers.

FINAL EXPLORATION OF THE TALES OF BEEDLE THE BARD

It takes some years for a book to find its place in the canon of literature, and at least a generation for a rounded assessment to emerge. Yet even at the outset some comments can be offered.

There are of course weaknesses in this book:

It is far too short. Long-distance readers of the seven Harry Potter novels want something which takes more than an hour to read.

It does not mention Harry Potter and contributes relatively little to expanding the world of Harry Potter.

There are mistakes in it. J. K. Rowling's misuses of the English words *translation* and *warlock* are both beyond defense, especially in a book which must have benefited from the most careful editorial over-view and proof-reading.

There are plot weaknesses, particularly in *The Warlock's Hairy Heart* and *Babbitty Rabbitty and her Cackling Stump*.

This book is not perfect, and may well disappoint many fans.

There can be no doubt that J. K. Rowling is a good writer. In the Harry Potter books she presents seven gripping stories, brilliantly told, and set within a rich and complex world created from her imagination. Similarly there can be no doubt that the Harry Potter phenomenon has gripped the English speaking world, and we are seeing an unparalleled literary event. Yet there is a big step from good writer and marketing phenomenon to the ranks of the greats. Before reading *The Tales of Beedle the Bard* I was certain that J. K. Rowling had not taken this step. Now I'm a little less sure.

There are moments in her Harry Potter books when a feature suggests a writer good even in the company of other good writers.

There are also moments in her books when she produces work not up to her usual standard. As is the case with all writers, her work is uneven in quality, but at its best it is very good indeed. In the final book *Harry Potter and the Deathly Hallows* J. K. Rowling produces something that is good throughout, and in places truly outstanding. Whether her readers know it (and I think most probably don't), *Harry Potter and the Deathly Hallows* is an outstanding Christian book written by a committed Christian. Its hero lives his life in accordance with the promptings of love, even to the extent of calmly accepting his own death to save those around him. In as much as it is a Christian novel this is great literature, but while the Christian allegory is readily seen in such novels as C. S. Lewis's *The Lion, the Witch and the Wardrobe* it is here hidden to the extent that most readers do not realise what they are reading. In its exploration of a Christian life *Harry Potter and the Deathly Hallows* is outstanding. In not pointing the allegory so that all readers may understand it, it falls short of great.

If the good writer J. K. Rowling has a claim to greatness, that claim must rest on *The Tales of Beedle the Bard*. Stories this short are a difficult genre, and to write a tale of a thousand words or thereabouts which truly holds the reader's attention is a considerable achievement.

My view is that two of her tales are not wholly successful, and may even be considered to fail. They may entertain for a few minutes, but I cannot see how they can endure. *The Wizard and the Hopping Pot* is amusing, but the tale is unsatisfactory in that there is no sense of the young wizard having learnt his lesson. *Babbitty Rabbitty and her Cackling Stump* is far too complicated, and lacking a clear message. This leaves three tales which seem to me to be something very special.

The Warlock's Hairy Heart I find unsettling. It is a blood-drenched horror, and the uncompromising despair of the world it presents is deeply disturbing. This isn't a story for children. It isn't a nice story. It offends. I don't think J. K. Rowling should have written it, let alone published it. I don't like it at all. But I think it is a very powerful piece of writing indeed. Maybe it should be regarded as an antidote to the sugar-coated view of the world presented by virtually all writing for children. Maybe it takes us a step further along the road to understanding the world we live in through its blunt depiction of evil in the world. This is the theology of the devil unchained, allowed to work his mischief in our world, and to get this into a tale this short is a signal achievement.

The Tale of the Three Brothers has that rare capacity in a short piece of writing of provoking thought. As the skull motif at the beginning of this story and on the cover of the book indicate it is a tale about death. J. K. Rowling does not shirk this topic. Indeed it is a theme of all the Harry Potter books. In their youth the three brothers have an encounter with Death, and they respond in different ways. The first two seek to control death. The elder brother tries to do this through his own power—much as Voldemort does in the Harry Potter novels. The middle brother seeks control through suicide—not explored in the Harry Potter novels. The third lives a full life, and when his life is over accepts his death, greeting Death as an old friend. J. K. Rowling seems to be asking us to contemplate death, be it our own or that of people around us, with acceptance.

The Fountain of Fair Fortune is a neat and satisfying story around positive values. Co-operation with others, consideration for others, and ultimately love for others, allow all four to find happiness, and to find it within themselves.

We have three excellent stories around the potent themes of evil, death and love. We also have a marketing phenomenon. Sales of *The Tales of Beedle the Bard* are in their millions. These stories have the potential to be the new fairy stories of a new generation. If

J. K. Rowling really has brought about a situation where her remarkable stories are the tales told to children and remembered for a lifetime then she has indeed crossed the line from being merely a good writer to being great.

FURTHER READING

Great to read now:

The Unauthorized Harry Potter Quiz Book

Re-Read Harry Potter and the Sorcerer's Stone *Today*

Re-Read Harry Potter and the Chamber of Secrets *Today*

Forthcoming 2009:

Re-Read Harry Potter and the Prisoner of Azkaban *Today*

Re-Read Harry Potter and the Goblet of Fire *Today*

Re-Read Harry Potter and the Order of the Phoenix *Today*

Re-Read Harry Potter and the Half Blood Prince *Today*

Re-Read Harry Potter and the Deathly Hallows *Today*

All by Graeme Davis and all published by Nimble Books LLC, and all available from online booksellers everywhere or via http://www.NimbleBooks.com.

NIMBLE BOOKS LLC

NIMBLE BOOKS LLC

www.ingramcontent.com/pod-product-compliance
Lightning Source LLC
Chambersburg PA
CBHW081325020726
47506CB00005B/1179